LSCA TITLE I

Cancer

UNDERSTANDING
ILLNESS

Cancer

Elaine Landau

TWENTY-FIRST CENTURY BOOKS

A Division of Henry Holt and Company
New York

Twenty-First Century Books
A Division of Henry Holt and Company, Inc.
115 West 18th Street
New York, NY 10011

Henry Holt ® and colophon are trademarks of
Henry Holt and Company, Inc.
Publishers since 1866

Published in Canada by Fitzhenry & Whiteside Ltd.,
195 Allstate Parkway, Markham, Ontario, L3R 4T8

Library of Congress Cataloging-in-Publication Data
Landau, Elaine.
Cancer / Elaine Landau. — 1st ed.
p. cm. — (Understanding illness)
Includes bibliographical references and index.
1. Cancer—Juvenile literature. [1. Cancer. 2. Diseases.]
I. Title. II Series: Landau, Elaine. Understanding illness.
RC264.L36 1994
616.99'4—dc20   94-13844
                                                                  CIP
                                                                  AC

ISBN 0-8050-2990-7
First Edition 1994

Printed in the United States of America
All first editions are printed on acid-free paper ∞.
10 9 8 7 6 5 4 3 2 1

Photo Credits
p. 13: David Lane/*Palm Beach Post*; p. 17: Visuals Unlimited/David
M. Phillips; p. 18: Visuals Unlimited; p. 20: John S. Stewart/Ozark
Stock; p. 24: David M. Grossman; pp. 25, 27, 29: Harvey Finkle/Alan
Hinerfeld/Preferred Stock; pp. 32, 34, 51: National Cancer Institute;
p. 37: Visuals Unlimited/F. Sloop–W. Ober; p. 39: Tony Freeman/
PhotoEdit; p. 42: John S. Stewart/Ozark Stock; p. 45: Seth Resnick/
Light Sources, Stock; p. 46: Neena Wilmot/Stock/Art Images; p. 53:
Janet Century/PhotoEdit; p. 55 (both): Amy C. Etra/PhotoEdit.

For Brenna Tudor

CONTENTS

Cancer

Cancer

There's a children's camp in the Southwest that at first glance looks very much like any other camp for young people. Surrounded by mosquitoes, musty tents, a baseball field, hiking trail, lake, swimming pond, and arts and crafts area, campers remain happily busy throughout the day. Evenings are generally spent sitting around the campfire, toasting marshmallows, listening to scary stories, and singing songs. As might be expected a summer doesn't pass without at least a few humorous pranks— including campers hiding an assortment of creepy crawling creatures in their counselors' beds.

Yet a closer look reveals that this camp isn't quite typical of similar summer havens across America. Here at any given time you're likely to find a number of the campers' artificial limbs and wheelchairs neatly stacked in a spacious room at the facility. There's also a mandatory activity known as medication period that rarely occurs at other camps. At about 2:30 P.M. each day campers canoeing in the lake row to shore while those hiking in the surrounding woods start back. Clay figures and pottery are left on craft tables while everyone heads for the infirmary.

As one camp staffer described what occurs, "No one

has to call them. They know. It's med time. They push open the door and leave their childhood behind."[1] Besides spending the summer learning to dive and swim, shoot arrows, or mark a trail, these campers are actively engaged in a life or death struggle—they have cancer. Their fight for survival sometimes means interrupting pleasant activities to take unpleasant drugs or undergo other necessary medical procedures. Yet they accept med time as an inescapable part of their day. A counselor described how one young boy handled the situation this way: "His ten-year-old size conflicts with his technical expertise. He has the ability to scan blood reports with the same rapid comprehension that his peers might scan comic books. When his plastic tray is presented to him, he explains to the nurse the procedure while she listens intently. Each tray is a parent's hope, a child's future."[2]

In a matter of moments the treatment is over and the boy goes back to being a child. That afternoon he may run a relay race, go to a local petting zoo with his counselor and friends, or chase girls around the field, trying to pull their ponytails.

As these children face down cancer, their optimism and uncanny ability to make the most of each day are inspiring. In many cases having a life-threatening illness has forced them to develop coping skills and a positive attitude essential to triumphing over a potentially devastating disease. As one 17-year-old cancer patient wrote:

"Face it. You've got to be like me to really appreciate how silly it is to read a letter in Dear Abby's column about a woman upset because her neighbor hasn't returned her salad bowls. It's like, 'Ooooh lady, how can you stand it?' One of my philosophies is that you know

Being able to join in the fun with friends helps
a patient through the difficult stages of recovery.

it's happening, so you might as well laugh with it. If I were serious about the situation all the time, I'd be crying all the time. Who wants that?"[3]

Cancer. To most people it's still a frightening word. This attitude may go back to what it was like to have cancer in the past. During the early part of this century a cancer diagnosis was like getting a death sentence. At the time, cancer was recognized as a major killer and doctors knew very little about its causes and even less about cures for the disease. Surgery was the only recognized cancer treatment, but for surgery to be effective, it had to be performed in the early stages of the illness. Since patients often did not know or recognize cancer's warning signs, large numbers of them died.

As if the disease alone weren't bad enough, there was also a stigma attached to having cancer. The lack of public knowledge about the illness gave rise to negative stereotypes. Some people wrongly believed that cancer was contagious and therefore tried to avoid those with the disease. People hesitated to tell their employers that they had cancer for fear of being fired. Often when a family member had cancer, relatives kept it a secret—not wanting to be known as "a cancer family." Even obituaries whitewashed cancer deaths, stating that the person died of an unnamed lingering illness.

Today the situation has dramatically changed. Scientists have learned a great deal about cancer, and new lifesaving and life-extending treatments have been developed. Our knowledge about cancer prevention and early detection has significantly broadened as well.

Old attitudes have begun to change in response to the growing number of people who are surviving cancer. In the 1930s only one out of every five cancer patients lived for five or more years following their diagnosis. But now more than half the cancer patients pass that mark. The figures are especially promising for young people. Some of the cancers that primarily affect children have fairly high cure rates. The National Cancer Institute reports that 63 percent of young cancer patients now pass the five-year mark as compared to only 40 percent in 1970.[4]

In addition, many patients presently take a more active role in determining their treatment plans. Today cancer is still a serious disease, but survival rates continue to improve. This book is about cancer—the challenges it presents and the medical as well as personal battles waged to conquer it.

Sometimes learning about cancer or any other serious illness can be a little unsettling. After reading this book don't hesitate to discuss any feelings you may have with your doctor, parents, or another important adult in your life.

CHAPTER TWO

Is It Cancer?

Cancer is a term used to describe a group of more than 100 related diseases. These illnesses are similar in that each is a disease of the body's cells. However, their names differ—there's lung cancer, breast cancer, leukemia, Hodgkin's disease, non-Hodgkin's lymphoma, et cetera—and various types of cancer may require different treatments. There are also differences in the survival rates.

The human body is composed of millions of tiny cells. Under normal conditions the different types of cells, such as skin cells, hair cells, or blood cells, act in an orderly, predictable manner to allow the body to maintain itself. Cells continually create new cells by dividing in two. This way worn-out cells are replaced by new, healthy ones.

However, sometimes cells lose their ability to direct and control their growth. They may divide too rapidly and reproduce in a haphazard fashion. In some types of cancer the bulk of tissue produced as a result is known as a tumor. There are two types of tumors—benign and malignant.

Benign tumors tend not to be dangerous. Unlike cancer cells they do not spread to other parts of the body and in most cases aren't life threatening. Often tumors can be

16

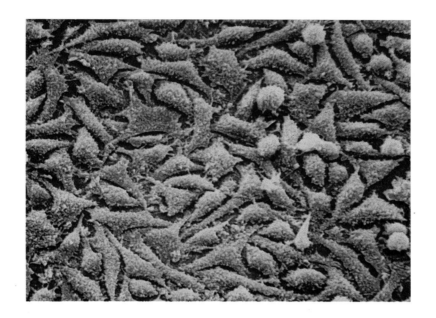

*Rapidly dividing
cancer cells*

surgically removed and do not return. Malignant tumors, on the other hand, are cancerous. Groups of cells from these tumors may break away and travel through the bloodstream or lymphatic system to other parts of the body. When cancer cells spread, or metastasize, they form new tumors. Malignant tumors invade and destroy nearby tissues and organs.

Since arresting or stopping cancer involves catching the disease in its early stages, it's important to know its symptoms. The National Cancer Institute cites the following conditions as the most common warning signs of cancer:

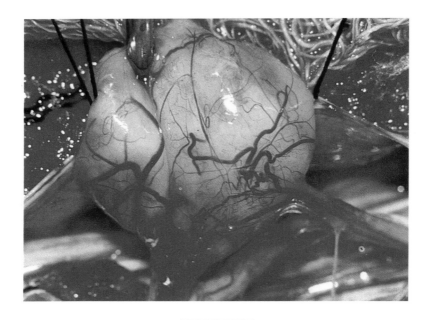

*A malignant tumor removed
from a patient with cancer.*

- a change in bowel or bladder habits,
- a sore that doesn't heal,
- unusual bleeding or discharge,
- a thickening or lump in the breast or elsewhere,
- frequent indigestion or problems swallowing,
- an obvious change in a wart or mole,
- a persistent cough or hoarseness.

Having one or more of these problems does not necessarily mean that a person has cancer. Each could indicate a less distressing medical condition. However, if any of the above symptoms lasts for two or more weeks, the individual should see a doctor. It's important not to delay. Many people wait until a symptom becomes painful even though pain is not an early warning sign of cancer.

Besides knowing cancer's early warning signs, both males and females should have regularly scheduled physical exams. Fortunately, early detection tests for some types of cancer have been developed that allow a doctor to identify the disease even before symptoms appear. These tests assist doctors in diagnosing cancer of the colon, rectum, mouth, skin, breast, cervix, prostate, and testicles at an early stage. They are as follows:

EXAMINATIONS FOR BOTH MALES AND FEMALES

COLON AND RECTUM EXAM

In performing this procedure a doctor inserts a gloved finger into the rectum and gently probes for lumps. Every three to five years patients more than 50 years of age should also be rectally examined with an instrument called a sigmoidoscope—a tubelike tool used to examine a portion of the colon.[1]

In addition, after turning 50, everyone should have a yearly test to check for blood in the stool (the matter discharged during a bowel movement). Blood in the stool can be a sign of colon cancer. However, as this can also indicate other conditions, further tests are necessary before a final diagnosis can be determined.

MOUTH EXAMINATION

It's important for dentists to thoroughly examine their patients' mouths for signs of cancer at regular intervals. Individuals should use a mirror monthly to examine their

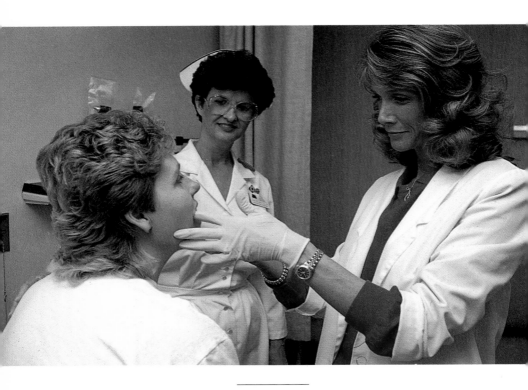

A specialist on diseases of the mouth carefully checks her patient for early signs of cancer.

own mouths as well. They should note any changes in the color of the gums, lips, or cheeks. Scabs, cracks, sores, swelling, bleeding, or thickening in any part of the mouth can indicate a problem as well. While none of these specific changes is a certain sign of cancer, they should nevertheless be checked by a dentist or physician.

SKIN EXAMINATION

Everyone should check their skin regularly for signs of new growths or other skin changes. A difference in the color and shape of a mole or a developing cyst should be promptly reported to a physician. In addition to self-examination doctors should look over their patients' skin during medical checkups.

EXAMINATIONS FOR WOMEN

BREAST EXAMINATION

All women should learn to perform breast self-examination (BSE) and do this on a monthly basis. The women will be checking for unusual changes such as a lump or a thickening of tissue. Breast self-examination is especially important for women more than 40 years old since the risk of breast cancer rises with age. If a woman notices a lump or other change in her breast, she should immediately see a doctor. While 80 percent of all breast lumps are not malignant, only a doctor can make a certain diagnosis.

Women more than 40 years of age should have a mammogram every one to two years. A mammogram is a breast X ray that can reveal tumors or other breast changes too small to be detected even by a thorough physical examination.

CERVIX EXAMINATION

Early detection of cervical cancer (cancer of the lower, narrow end of the uterus) is extremely important. Women should have regularly scheduled pelvic examinations and Pap tests. To perform a Pap test, a doctor takes a sample of cells from the upper vagina and cervix with a cotton swab or wooden scraper. These cells are placed on a glass slide and examined under a microscope. A Pap test detects cervical cancer as well as the cell changes that precede it. Women should begin having Pap tests after turning 18 or once they become sexually active.

EXAMINATIONS FOR MEN

PROSTATE EXAMINATION

The prostate is a gland of the male reproductive system lying just below the bladder. A rectal examination by a doctor is considered the most reliable way to detect early prostate cancer because an irregular or unusually hard area might signal the presence of a tumor. Difficulty in urination may also be a warning sign. Ideally such examinations should be included in yearly physicals for males more than 40 years old.

TESTICLE EXAMINATION

The testicles are two egg-shaped glands in the male's scrotum. These glands are part of the male reproductive system and secrete male hormones. Testicular cancer most commonly occurs among men between 24 and 34 years of age. In the majority of cases it is discovered by men performing monthly testicular self-examination (TSE). If while examining himself a man notices a lump or an enlargement of the testicles, unusual soreness, tenderness, or pain, he should see his physician. A testicle examination by a doctor should be part of annual medical checkups as well.

Unfortunately there aren't any early detection tests targeting cancers such as non-Hodgkin's lymphoma and acute lymphocytic leukemia, which most commonly affect young people. Non-Hodgkin's lymphoma begins in the lymph cells but generally results in tumors of the abdomen, bone marrow, or chest. While both girls and boys can get this type of cancer, it is three times more common among young males. Symptoms often entail coughing and difficulty breathing in cases in which the thymus gland becomes enlarged. If a tumor develops in the abdominal area, pain and swelling may result, while there's frequently vomiting if a tumor forms in the bowel.

Acute lymphocytic leukemia (ALL) is characterized by the abnormal development of a type of white blood cells (immature lymphocytes) that collect in the bone marrow, bloodstream, and lymphatic system. ALL symptoms can either appear suddenly or come on slowly and may include high fever, chills, respiratory discomfort, swollen lymph nodes, an enlarged spleen or liver, bruising and bleeding easily, bone or joint pain, weakness, and irritability. Sometimes called "childhood leukemia," ALL usually strikes children between the ages of two and nine.

Once one or more possible symptoms appears for any type of cancer, the person's doctor will need additional information to arrive at an accurate diagnosis. Usually this includes the patient's medical history, a thorough physical examination, and more tests. Besides the standard X rays used to learn about what's happening inside the body, at times special types of X rays are used to detect cancer as well as various other diseases.

Among these is the CAT (computerized axial tomography) scan, which provides the doctor with a computerized three-dimensional picture of the body. Another helpful test in detecting tumors uses radioactive isotopes

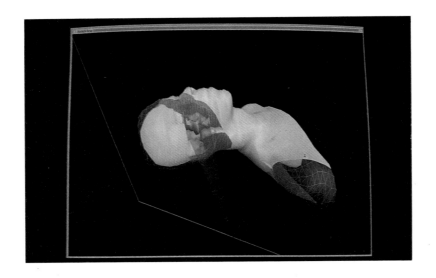

A CAT scan of a cancer patient.
The cancerous area is shown in red.

to identify abnormal growths. Here the patient either
swallows or is injected with a mild radioactive material.
The substance is then tracked with specially designed
devices to enable physicians to pinpoint the tumor.

Ultrasound is sometimes also used as a diagnostic
tool to detect cancer. In such cases high-frequency sound
waves are aimed at a particular part of the patient's body.
These waves bounce off the tissues and organs, forming a
picture on a screen that allows doctors to see abnormal
growths. Besides these tests, several laboratory diagnostic procedures may be performed. Certain blood and
urine tests can provide doctors with additional useful
information. However, the only positive way to tell if a
patient has cancer is through a biopsy. During a biopsy

*During a biopsy part or all of the
growth is removed for further testing.*

either the whole tumor or a portion of it is surgically removed. The growth is then examined under a microscope for cancer cells.

After it's determined that the patient has cancer, the doctor must see if the cancer cells have spread. To do so, further tests are performed, revealing the stage of the disease. At that point the doctor will be armed with the information needed to devise the best treatment plan for the patient.

CHAPTER THREE

Treatment

Treating cancer has come a long way in recent years. Much of the success is due to improved diagnostic and treatment methods. Yet regardless of the hope new treatments promise, cancer is still a difficult illness to deal with.

Nevertheless that's what the Williams family (name changed) had to do when five-year-old Peter became ill. The young boy had been looking forward to a fun-filled year when it happened. He was anxious to start kindergarten that fall and was especially excited about finally being old enough to play in a junior baseball league.

But in May Peter began having stomachaches. His parents took the boy to his pediatrician and, later on, to a urologist. Neither physician could find anything wrong with him. However, during a baseball game the following month Peter doubled over with cramps and his father had to carry him off the field. When the pain returned two days later, Peter's parents brought him to Children's Hospital in Oklahoma City, Oklahoma. The facility was more than 100 miles (160 kilometers) from their home, but the Williamses wanted the best possible care for their child.

Unfortunately, it wasn't long before they heard some

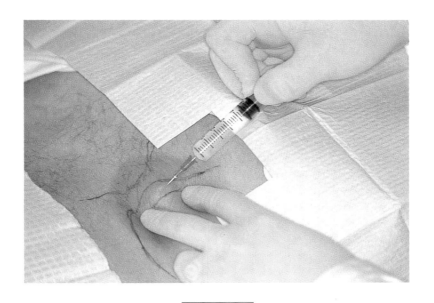

A bone marrow biopsy, or aspiration

bad news. The doctor who examined Peter felt a growth and the X rays taken revealed that he had a tumor. The family wouldn't have a final diagnosis for several days, until a CAT scan and biopsy could be done, but the physicians strongly suspected cancer.

Soon afterward, the Williamses heard the news they dreaded. Their son was a very sick little boy. Peter had Burkitt's lymphoma—a cancer of the lymph glands known to advance quickly in children. There were signs that Peter's cancer had already spread somewhat. To see if his cancer had spread to the bone, the doctors performed a procedure known as bone marrow aspiration. They inserted a needle into Peter's hip to withdraw a sample of the spongy material that fills the bone cavities.

The cancer hadn't reached the bone, which improved his chances of surviving. But despite this positive sign the Williamses knew that their fight was far from over. The doctors told the Williamses that Burkitt's lymphoma can sometimes be cured but they didn't offer any odds. Peter's family could only hope for the best.

The coming days were frightening for the Williamses. Peter's weight had already dropped from 50 to 33 pounds (23 to 15 kilograms) and they didn't know how much his small body could endure. If the five-year-old was to recover, he'd have to respond favorably to chemotherapy.

Fortunately, Peter did. The doctors noted a dramatic improvement after just the first treatment and by the end of the chemotherapy cycle, Peter's cancer was in remission. Remission means the temporary or permanent disappearance of the disease's symptoms. His family was thrilled with Peter's improvement and his mother joyfully recalled that before long her son was well enough to leave his hospital bed for a ride in the playroom's small red wagon.

Peter left the hospital two weeks later while continuing his treatment as an outpatient. But although they hoped the worst was over, things still weren't easy for Peter and his family. After only being home a few days he suffered a severe stomachache and leg cramps. The child was rushed to the hospital, where he had a seizure. For a few seconds afterward one side of Peter's body went limp and he did not even recognize his mother.

Peter's family feared that the boy's tumor was back. However, the doctor's reassured them that Peter had had some of the negative side effects of chemotherapy. The

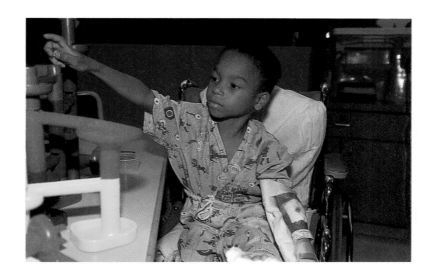

A young cancer patient, like Peter Williams, undergoing chemotherapy

physicians adjusted the boy's medication accordingly and Peter was able to return home.

As the months passed, Peter regained his strength. Although there had been the possibility of kidney damage, it never occurred. And soon Peter began behaving as he had before having cancer. He rode his bike, played ball, and served as the ring bearer at his uncle's wedding. It was impossible to forget that Peter had cancer, since the boy's chemotherapy and bone marrow work had to continue for seven months. But by February the treatments were over and that spring he eagerly looked forward to playing baseball.

Peter Williams proved to be an asset to his junior league team. At the annual tournament that June they only needed one more run to win when Peter was up at bat. Although he missed the first ball, the now able-bodied boy batted in the winning run moments later. The winning streak continued as Peter's future medical checkups showed him to be cancer-free. Peter did more than just help his ball team—he defeated the disease that had threatened his life.

The children described in chapter one and Peter Williams are inspiring examples of personal strength and endurance. But much of their success in overcoming cancer had to do with current medical advances. A patient's progress often depends on the type of cancer, how far it has spread, and how he or she responds to treatment. All cancer treatment plans are tailored to the patient's medical history, age, and general health.

There are several ways to tackle cancer. Some are local treatments that strive to eliminate the cancer in a particular part of the body. Surgery is considered a local treatment as it entails removing cancer cells from a single area. Systemic treatments, on the other hand, involve the patient's entire bodily system. These include anticancer drugs that enter the bloodstream and are carried throughout the body. At times a physician may rely on one or more types of treatment, depending on the circumstances. Those most routinely used are described below.

SURGERY

In cancer surgery the tumor is removed as is a portion of the surrounding tissues that may contain cancer cells. At times healthy surrounding tissue may also have to be removed to insure that the cancer doesn't spread.

Following surgery the patient may be in some discomfort. There may be soreness surrounding the wound and, if any nerves were cut, the patient may have numbness or tingling in the area as well. Many individuals also feel tired or weak for a time afterward, but reactions differ among patients.

RADIATION THERAPY

Radiation therapy, another type of local cancer treatment, is sometimes also called X-ray therapy, radiotherapy, cobalt therapy, or irradiation. High-energy rays are aimed at a specific group of cancer cells, severely damaging them so the cells can't grow and multiply in the body. Radiation therapy is often used in combination with surgery. It may be done prior to surgery to shrink the tumor to be removed or afterward to destroy any cancer cells remaining after the operation.

The two forms of radiation used are called external radiation therapy and radiation implants.

EXTERNAL RADIATION THERAPY

In external radiation therapy a machine directs high-energy rays at the cancerous area. These treatments are generally given five days a week for several weeks. Patients receiving external radiation therapy usually do not stay in the hospital but instead go there for their treatments.

RADIATION IMPLANTS

Patients receiving radiation implants have a small container of radioactive material placed in the body cavity or

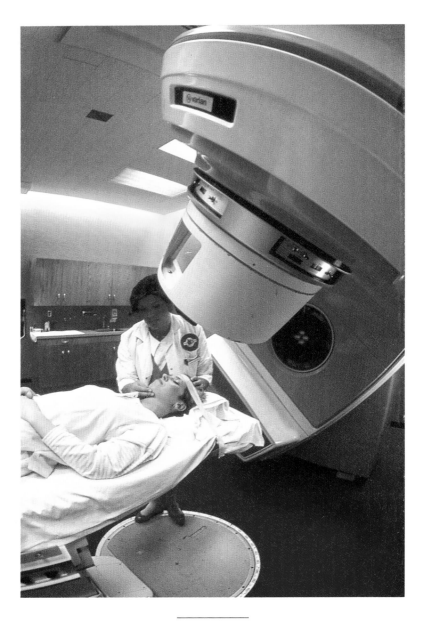

A patient undergoing radiation treatment for cancer.

directly into the cancer itself. Doctors use this method in treating specific parts of the body when it's best to place the cancer-killing rays very close to the tumor. Radiation implants also permit physicians to administer an extremely high dose of radiation without harming the healthy tissue near the cancerous area.

Patients who receive radiation implants usually remain in the hospital in isolated rooms during treatment. Throughout this time a thick protective shield is placed around their beds and hospital personnel have limited contact with them. That's because the radioactive material in the patient can transmit rays to the surrounding area. However, as soon as the implant is removed, the patient is no longer radioactive and there's no danger of contamination.

The common side effects of radiation therapy include exhaustion and rashes or red blotches on the area of the body being treated. At times there may also be a drop in the patient's white blood cell count (white blood cells fight infection). These reactions are not permanent and disappear when the treatment is over.

CHEMOTHERAPY

In chemotherapy, a systemic treatment, the patient is given drugs designed to destroy cancer cells. Different drugs administered in various ways are used for this purpose. Some are swallowed by the patient, while others are injected into a muscle, vein, or artery.

At times chemotherapy is done in cycles. The patients take the drugs for a specified time before discontinuing the medication and later starting it again.

*Chemotherapy being administered
through an IV (intravenous injection).*

Depending on the patient and the type of drug used, chemotherapy may be given at a doctor's office, a hospital, or the patient's home.

Unfortunately, chemotherapy patients often endure unpleasant side effects such as hair loss, diarrhea, mouth sores, nausea and vomiting, and weakness.[1] Some chemotherapy drugs also decrease the bone marrow's ability to produce blood cells, making the patient more vulnerable to infections.

HORMONE THERAPY

Some cancers, such as those of the breast, prostate, kidney, and uterus, depend on hormones to grow and spread. In these instances the doctor may try to block the body's production of the particular hormone with drugs or surgically remove the hormone-producing organ.

Depending on the type of hormone therapy used, the patient may have various side effects. These include nausea and vomiting as well as swelling or weight gain.

IMMUNOTHERAPY, OR BIOLOGICAL THERAPY

This form of therapy is the newest type of cancer treatment available. Here natural and man-made substances are used to boost or specifically direct the patient's immune system (the cells and organs that defend the body against infection and disease). One such substance, called interferon, stimulates the immune system to fight cancer cells while another, known as Interleukin-2, regulates cell growth to inhibit the cancer's spread.

There are presently more than five million people in the United States who have had some form of cancer. Many owe their lives to the cancer treatments discussed here. However, even when a patient's symptoms disappear following treatment, doctors often hesitate to say that person has been cured. Unfortunately, the disease sometimes reappears at a later time. Therefore, cancer patients must be carefully monitored to detect any return of the illness.

In the majority of cases a person who has remained symptom-free for five years is considered cured. As researchers continue to seek new and better methods of fighting cancer, the odds for recovery are expected to grow.

CHAPTER FOUR

Cancer:
Causes and Prevention

No one is certain why one person gets cancer and another does not. Nevertheless researchers today know much more about the disease than they did in the past. They know that someone cannot get cancer due to an accident or injury. Cells do not turn cancerous because someone had a bad fall or was in an automobile crash. Scientists also know that cancer isn't contagious. You cannot "catch" cancer from another person regardless of whether you swim in the same pool, eat lunch together, or sit next to each other at work or school.

Studies of cancer patients revealed that while both young and old people develop the disease, cancer is more likely to strike middle-aged or elderly individuals. Cancer is currently declining among women and rising among men. If it continues to occur at its present rate, approximately 30 percent of the U.S. population, or 73 million Americans alive today, will eventually develop some form of this disease. This means that as time passes someone in three out of every four families will have cancer.[1]

The debate over precisely how someone develops cancer continues. But many scientists believe that it occurs as a result of continued contact with cancer-

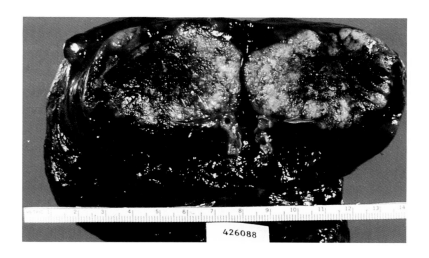

Smokers are at a high risk for
lung cancer (shown above).

causing agents called carcinogens. These researchers suspect that cancer begins through a double-phased process
involving two types of agents, known as initiators and
promoters. Initiators are the first-phase culprits. These
agents begin the damage to a cell that eventually results
in cancer. In lung cancer cases, for example, cigarette
smoking has proven to be an initiator.

Promoters generally do not cause cancer on their
own. Instead, they turn cells already damaged by an initiator into cancer cells. Therefore, someone who smokes
heavily may be prone to cancer of the mouth, with tobacco as the initiator. If that person drinks as well, the alcohol further enables the cancer to develop. So in this
instance alcohol is the promoter.

In recent years scientists have identified a number of

elements that place people at high risk for cancer. Many cancer cases are related to outside environmental factors as well as to what people eat, drink, and smoke. By purposely avoiding the risks described below, an individual can help guard against cancer.

TOBACCO

Smoking has clearly been shown to cause cancer. A smoker is ten times more likely than a nonsmoker to get cancer. Smoking is also responsible for 30 percent of all cancer-related deaths. Smokers' risk levels vary according to the kind and amount of cigarettes or cigars they smoke, how deeply they inhale, and how long they've been smoking. Besides lung cancer, smokers also have a greater chance than people who don't smoke of developing cancer of the mouth, throat, esophagus, pancreas, and bladder. New evidence also indicates that smoking may be linked to cancer of the stomach.

Chewing tobacco and oral snuff, sometimes referred to as "smokeless" tobacco, are not safer choices. These products cause cancer of the mouth and pharynx (the upper portion of the throat just behind the mouth). However, smokers and people who use chewing tobacco and oral snuff should not continue their habit thinking that the damage is already done. As soon as a person stops using some form of tobacco, the cancer risk decreases.

"Passive smoking," or breathing in other people's cigarette smoke within an enclosed space, is another serious concern. Working or attending classes in a smoky environment raises a person's chances of getting cancer. According to the American Thoracic Society of the

Unfortunately, in recent years chewing tobacco has become increasingly popular among some young people.

American Lung Association, "Secondhand smoke causes cancer in humans and is responsible for an estimated 3,000 lung cancer deaths annually among nonsmokers in the United States."[2]

DIET

The type and amount of food people eat have a bearing on their chances of getting cancer. Researchers now suspect that a third of all cancer deaths are related to our food intake. High-fat diets especially have been linked to cancer of the breast, colon, prostate, and endometrium (the lining of the uterus). Being extremely overweight has been tied to higher death rates among those suffering from prostate, pancreatic, breast, and ovarian cancer as well. Other studies show that people who eat pickled, cured, or smoked foods have a greater chance of developing stomach cancer.

Nutritionists stress that eating a healthy, well-balanced diet lowers a person's cancer risk. To help people maintain good eating habits, the U.S. Department of Agriculture and the Department of Health and Human Services offer the following guidelines:

Eat a variety of foods. This is important to obtain the nutrients necessary for good health and a sound body. Be sure to include fruits and vegetables rich in vitamins A and C and beta-carotene, since they reduce the risk of some types of cancer. Dark green leafy vegetables and the red, yellow, and orange fruits and vegetables are good choices.

Maintain a desirable weight. Obesity is a risk factor for some cancers.

Avoid too much fat and cholesterol. A low-fat diet reduces the risk of some cancers as well as heart disease. When preparing meat, trim away the fat before eating it. If possible, choose poultry dishes, such as turkey and chicken, instead of red meat. The skin and any fat should be removed before cooking these items. Select low-fat dairy products rather than those made with whole milk or cream. For snacks replace pastries and deep-fried foods with fresh fruits and vegetables and air-popped popcorn.

The way food is cooked also determines its fat content. Meats should be cooked on racks that allow fats to drip off. Fats should also be drained from the pan before preparing gravy. Rely on herbs, spices, and lemon juice for seasoning instead of fats and salt. Low-fat microwavable pizzas and various low-fat frozen dinners and desserts are available at most supermarkets. Some fast-food restaurants also offer salad bars as an alternative to their less healthful choices.

Eat foods with adequate starch and fiber. Many nutritionists believe Americans should increase the level of starch and fiber in their diets by eating more potatoes, pastas, whole grain breads and cereals, and legumes (dried peas and beans). A high-fiber diet lessens the risk of colon and rectal cancer.

Avoid too much sugar. Sugary foods are often high in fat and calories and low in important nutrients.

Avoid too much sodium (a compound abundant in many foods that is essential to life).

Drink alcoholic beverages in moderation (for those of legal drinking age).[3] Excessive alcohol can lead to a number of serious health problems. Heavy drinking has been linked to cancer

A diet including vegetables and fruits rich in vitamins A, C, and beta-carotene (as shown above) can help lower a person's risk for some types of cancer.

of the mouth, throat, liver, and esophagus. As was mentioned earlier, the risk of cancer is especially high for people who both drink and smoke heavily.

X RAYS

People receiving large doses of radiation (as in X rays) increase their chances of developing cancer. While a single X ray only entails a small amount of radiation, repeated exposure to X rays can be hazardous. When seeing a doctor or dentist it's best to avoid X rays that aren't absolutely necessary. If X rays must be taken, shields should be used whenever possible to protect the rest of the body from radiation.

SUN EXPOSURE

People who sunbathe or are otherwise exposed to the sun increase their risk of developing skin cancer. This is especially true for people who have fair skin or freckle easily. As noted by Dr. Paul F. Engstrom, vice president, population science, FOX-CHASE Cancer Center in Philadelphia, "Essentially all of the more than 500,000 cases of skin cancer each year are caused by too much sun."[4]

The most harmful sun rays are called ultraviolet rays and are strongest during the summer months from about ten in the morning to three in the afternoon. During that period it is important to protect your skin if you're going to be in the sun. A hat, sunglasses, long pants, and a long-sleeve shirt can help block out harmful rays.

There are also sunscreens that are applied directly to the skin for sun protection. These products filter out ultraviolet rays, lessening the possibility of serious burns. The various sunscreens are rated by an SPF, or sun protection factor. An SPF of 8, for example, allows a person to stay in the sun eight times longer before burning than would be possible without using that sunscreen. The American Academy of Dermatology suggests that everyone use a sunscreen with an SPF of at least 15, although products with SPFs as high as 45 are available. Sadly many young people still mistakenly believe that a deep golden tan can harmlessly improve their appearance. But unseen skin damage from the sun at age 16 can turn into cancer within 60 years and show up as wrinkles or blotchy skin by the time the person is 30.

INDUSTRIAL AGENTS AND CHEMICALS

Being exposed to some industrial agents such as asbestos (formerly used as a building material) increases the risk of cancer. At times the industrial agents act alone; in other situations they heighten the effect of various environmental carcinogens. A smoker working in an asbestos-contaminated building would be at high risk for cancer.

Besides industrial agents that pollute the environment, being exposed to substantial amounts of household cleaning fluids, paint thinners, lawn and garden chemicals, and other similar products pose a cancer threat as well. Many such chemicals can be particularly hazardous if repeatedly inhaled in a poorly ventilated area. Therefore, it would not be wise to paint the interior of a house or disinfect a bathroom with the windows and door tightly shut.

In October 1993 environmentalists and women's groups united to launch a campaign against the use of chemicals made from chlorine. Recent research linked these substances to breast cancer. Unfortunately, chlorine-based chemicals can presently be found in a number of commonly used products such as clear plastic wrap, pesticides, and chlorine-bleached paper. According to a spokesperson for the campaign, "Studies have found that women with the highest amounts of these chemicals in their body have breast cancer risks from four to ten times higher than women with lower levels."[5]

The environmentalists and women's groups argued that there is no longer any need for chlorine pollution

Asbestos has been removed from many schools and buildings across the country. Here asbestos is eliminated from a school in a suburb of Boston, Massachusetts.

since "alternatives are available now for all major uses of chlorine." They further stressed that while a smattering of dangerous chemicals have been banned or restricted, many are still freely used.

Other groups have fought for additional research on the possible link between cancer and electromagnetic fields (EMFs). Electromagnetic fields, which can neither be seen nor heard, are generated by power lines and all electrical devices. EMFs have been a source of concern to many families since the release of a 1987 study suggesting a connection between electromagnetic fields and some forms of childhood cancer. In 1992 similar results were found by Sweden's Karolinska Institute. This led

*Exposure to extensive power lines
may be a cause of cancer.*

Sweden's National Board for Industrial and Technical
Development to compile a list of schools located near
high-voltage wires and to find out if the students were
negatively affected. In the United States similar monitor-
ing is being done at selected locations.

Unfortunately, some unusually high cancer rates
have already been detected among children in areas near
extensive power lines. This is expected to result in an

increasing array of nationwide legal challenges to electric utility companies. In San Diego, California, a couple sued the San Diego Gas and Electric Company, claiming that EMF lines above their house were responsible for their daughter's malignant kidney tumor. A comparable case was launched in Cape May, New Jersey.

In addition, utilities have met with increasing resistance from area residents when attempting to start a new power line or substation. In 1990 Jersey Central Power and Light Company (JCP&L) abandoned its intention to establish a major 10-mile (16-kilometer), 230-kilovolt transmission line in Monmouth County after strong protests from community members fearing exposure to EMFs. A host of similar demonstrations have followed.

HORMONES

Women taking the hormone estrogen to relieve the symptoms of menopause (sometimes called "change of life") or other conditions are believed to be at a higher risk for cancer of the uterus. There's also been a good deal of research to determine if taking oral contraceptives (birth control pills) can be cancer causing. A number of studies indicate that "the pill" does not increase a woman's chances of getting breast cancer and may actually lower the user's risk for cancer of the endometrium (the lining of the uterus) and ovaries.

Yet some scientists feel that those taking oral contraceptives may be at a greater risk for cancer of the cervix. Women considering any type of hormone treatment should discuss the pros and cons with their physician.

The risks discussed above are largely avoidable. However, some risk factors for cancer are out of the person's control. Individuals in the categories noted below have a higher-than-average chance of developing cancer.

People who have immediate family members or close relatives with melanoma (a virulent type of skin cancer), breast cancer, or cancer of the colon. These individuals are somewhat more likely to develop these cancers as well.

Individuals who had X-ray treatments to the head and neck as children or young teenagers for acne, enlargement of the thymus gland, or other conditions. These treatments may result in thyroid tumors, which can sometimes be malignant.

The daughters of women who took the drug diethylstilbestrol (DES) while they were pregnant. DES was given to pregnant women from the early 1940s to 1971. An estimated five to ten million females were exposed to it. DES and similar drugs have been linked to unusual tissue formations in the vagina and cervix of these women's daughters. The drug is also responsible for a rare type of vaginal and cervical cancer in a small number of DES daughters. The women who took DES themselves have been shown to be slightly more likely to develop breast cancer.

In all the instances described here, those at higher risk can best protect themselves by remaining alert to symptoms and having regular medical checkups.

CHAPTER FIVE

If It Happens . . .

Perhaps one of the most unsettling diagnoses a young person can hear is that he or she has cancer. Since all of us are individuals, there is bound to be a variety of reactions to the news. One teenage girl described her first response this way:

> When my doctor told me I had cancer, I started crying. I thought, Why did it have to happen to me? Why couldn't it be somebody else? A lot of other things flashed through my head. I was sure I was going to die. It was a real scary feeling. I worried about myself, and I worried about how my family was going to take it if something happened to me.
>
> When my doctor tried to tell me more about the cancer, I said, "Don't go any further because I don't want to hear any more." I kept thinking that I wasn't going to live much longer, so it didn't matter how much I knew.[1]

After the shock wears off, patients may feel stunned, angry, frightened, or a combination of these and other emotions. It's crucial that they allow himself time to adjust to what's happened and sort out their feelings. They may want to yell, cry, or brood for a while and all of these reactions are normal and acceptable. This is their way of coming to terms with an unpleasant and inescapable problem.

Once they've accepted what's occurred, it may be helpful to learn more about what to expect. Some find it useful to write their questions down for the doctor before their next appointment. If patients don't want to approach the physician alone, they should bring their parents or another older person they trust with them. Regardless of what they are told or read about the treatments ahead, it's important to remember that no two people are exactly alike and that everyone's body responds to prescribed therapies differently.

Anyone with cancer can expect to spend some time in the hospital as well as in clinics or doctors' offices. Being hospitalized and treated for cancer requires a considerable adjustment on a young person's part. There may be seemingly endless tests, schedules, X rays, special diets, and rules. Patients also have to get used to a host of doctors, nurses, therapists, and lab technicians who may sometimes seem to have taken over their lives.

At these times it may be useful to recall that the patient, his or her family, and the hospital staff are partners in restoring the ill person's health. Everyone needs to cooperate and honestly express what's on their mind. Even young patients can sometimes have a say about some aspects of their treatment. For example, in many cases chemotherapy or radiation treatments can be scheduled around the patients' needs, so they don't miss a special school event.

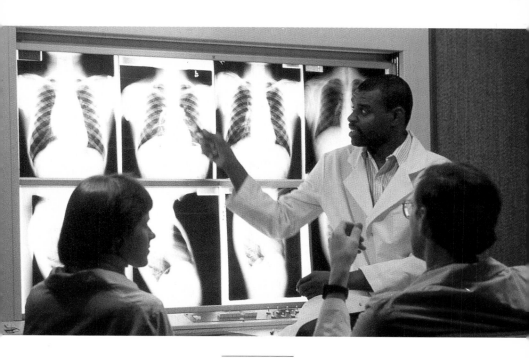

X rays (shown here) along with various other scans
and tests, may be useful in detecting cancer.

Every patient, regardless of age, has the right to be treated with respect and to express their feelings and concerns. Young patients for whom a particular situation is especially distressing may wish to discuss it with their doctor once they're calm and have collected their thoughts. Or they might prefer their parents, a nurse, or a hospital social worker to take up the matter with the physician instead. However, it's essential to set reasonable goals and not expect too much too soon. Everything can't always work out ideally and many times neither the patient nor the doctor is at fault.

Parents and other family members frequently are a good source of support for young cancer patients. Yet in a few cases the person's father or mother may find it especially hard to deal with the child's illness. Jack, a teen who had cancer, described his parent's reaction as follows: "My mother is taking over my life. Sometimes she acts like I'm two years old; other times like I'm ninety-two and can't do anything for myself."[2]

Parents who do more than necessary may merely be trying to help in a situation in which they feel powerless. Just as cancer patients experience a broad range of emotions, parents and brothers and sisters often do as well. Some parents blame themselves for their child's illness, even though they had nothing to do with it. The patient's siblings may feel sorry about their brother's or sister's cancer but at the same time resent the special attention and concern shown to him or her.

Most cancer patients are able to work through family difficulties that occur. It generally helps to talk about the problem and to respect the feelings of others involved. The patient also needs to let them know how they can best help. The patient should acknowledge good things they've done in the past and explain why these qualities are especially important now.

Going back to school and seeing old friends can sometimes also be troublesome for young cancer survivors. Although such situations may be awkward, classmates and friends tend to take their cues from the returning student. Depending on the circumstances, some people find it useful to explain what has occurred. Acquaintances and casual friends only need a brief explanation, but it may be comforting to share more information as well as feelings with close friends. As one girl who told her best friend what she'd been through described the experience: "When I first started chemotherapy, I explained it to my best friend. I told her that I

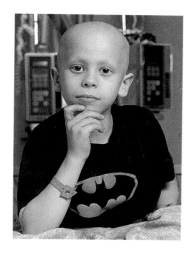

Chemotherapy can have many side effects, one of which is baldness. The hair will, however, eventually grow back again.

would probably be bald soon and that when I come home after treatment, [I'd be] sicker than a dog. She said, 'That's okay. I don't mind as long as you're you.'"[3]

Someone battling a serious illness deserves support but things don't always turn out that way. A young cancer survivor returning to school should be prepared to deal with some annoying questions. It may be necessary to assure classmates that cancer is not contagious and to repeatedly explain the physical changes resulting from some cancer treatments.

Ideally the ill person's friends should go out of their way to include him or her in activities, but unfortunately this isn't always the case, either. At first people may feel uncomfortable and not know what to say to someone who's had cancer. Therefore, the survivors should not be afraid to make the first move. When they feel well enough they might want to call friends to go to a movie, a mall, or watch a game together.

However, someone recovering from cancer should

not feel compelled to present a brave, smiling exterior. At times just getting through the day may seem like a major accomplishment. That's why it's important to know that there are people available to help. When immediate family members can't provide the needed time and attention, a grandparent, aunt, uncle, or close family friend may prove invaluable. Teachers and guidance counselors can also be helpful, even when the problem doesn't directly involve schoolwork. Some young cancer survivors feel comfortable talking to a clergyperson, while others prefer hospital social workers or psychologists.

Cancer support groups can also be extremely beneficial. Such groups for young people as well as older individuals have frequently been instrumental in assisting patients through some of the more difficult times. They are usually free of charge and provide a place where cancer patients can share their feelings with others who've had similar experiences. Cancer support groups are also often important sources of up-to-date information on the disease. Many groups invite cancer experts to speak at their meetings. Besides support groups for cancer patients, there are comparable groups for the parents and siblings of cancer victims as well as groups for children trying to cope with having a cancer-stricken parent.

When fighting cancer becomes especially difficult the person should remember that others have experienced the same feelings and have gone on to lead fulfilling lives. Perhaps the key lies in not losing sight of what's really important. As a young cancer survivor put it: "I have to say that there's been one positive result of my having cancer. It made me look at the real possibility of my own death, something I had never thought much

There are support groups for patients of all ages and their families. Knowing you are not alone always helps.

about before. That made me take a hard look at my life and decide what really mattered to me. As a survivor, I now see every day as a precious gift."[4]

It's sound advice for anyone—whether or not he or she has cancer.

E N D
NOTES

CHAPTER 1

1. Erma Bombeck, *I Want to Grow Hair, I Want to Grow Up, I Want to Go to Boise: Children Surviving Cancer* (New York: Harper & Row, 1989), xvi.

2. Ibid.

3. Ibid., xxi

4. Terence Monmaney and Eduardo Levy-Spira, "Young Survivors in a Deadly War," *Newsweek*, July 18, 1988, 50.

CHAPTER 2

1. Robert M. McAllister, M.D., Sylvia Teich Horowitz, Ph.D., and Raymond V. Gilden, Ph.D., *Cancer* (New York: Basic Books, 1993), 157.

CHAPTER 3

1. John Lazzlo, M.D., *Understanding Cancer* (New York: Harper & Row, 1987), 44.

CHAPTER 4

1. National Cancer Institute, *What You Need to Know about Cancer* (Bethesda, Md.: National Institutes of Health, 1989), 20.

2. American Thoracic Society, *"Facts about Secondhand Smoke"* (June 28, 1993), 1.

3. National Cancer Institute, *Diet, Nutrition, and Cancer Prevention: The Good News* (Bethesda, Md., National Institutes of Health, 1987), 1.

4. Steven Lally, "The Cancer Doctor's Anticancer Plan," *Prevention*, November 1990, 31.

5. "Environmentalists Link Breast Cancer to Chlorine," *Star-Ledger*, October 16, 1993.

CHAPTER 5

1. U.S. Department of Health and Human Services, *Help Yourself: Tips for Teens with Cancer* (Bethesda, Md. National Institutes of Health, 1990) 2.

2. Ibid., 25.

3. Ibid., 28.

4. U.S. Department of Health and Human Services, *Facing Forward: A Guide for Cancer Survivors* (Bethesda, Md.: National Institutes of Health, 1990), 15.

GLOSSARY

biopsy—the surgical removal of a growth or tissue sample to be examined under a microscope for cancer cells

carcinogen—a cancer-causing agent

chemotherapy—a cancer treatment that uses anticancer drugs

local treatment—a cancer therapy that only affects cells in the malignant (cancerous) tumor and surrounding area. Surgery is a local treatment for cancer.

lymphatic system—a network of small vessels that resemble blood vessels. The lymphatic system returns fluid from body tissues to the bloodstream.

mammogram—a breast X ray used for early cancer detection

metastasis—the spread of cancer from the malignant (cancerous) tumor (growth) to other parts of the body

radiation therapy—a cancer treatment that uses high-energy X rays or other sources of radiation

remission—the temporary or sometimes permanent disappearance of cancer symptoms

risk factor—an element that increases the chances of developing cancer

side effects—the mental and physical problems that some patients experience as a result of cancer treatments

sigmoidoscope—the tube-shaped instrument used by physicians to examine a portion of the colon

systemic treatment—a cancer treatment that affects cells throughout the body. An example of a systemic treatment is chemotherapy.

tumor—a tissue mass that is produced through abnormal cell division. Tumors can be benign (not cancerous) or malignant (cancerous).

FURTHER READING

Bergman, Thomas. *One Day at a Time: Children Living with Leukemia*. Milwaukee: Gareth Stevens Children's Books, 1989.

Fine, Judylaine. *Afraid to Ask: A Book for Families to Share about Cancer*. New York: Beech Tree Books, 1986.

Gravelle, Karen, and Bertram A. John. *Teenagers Face to Face with Cancer*. New York: Julian Messner, 1986.

Krementz, Jill. *How It Feels to Fight for Your Life*. Boston: Little Brown, 1989.

Monroe, Judy. *Leukemia*. New York: Crestwood House, 1990.

Silverstein, Alvin, and Virginia B. Silverstein. *Cancer: Can It Be Stopped?* New York: Lippincott, 1987.

Terkel, Susan Nelburg, and Marlene Lupiloff Brazz. *Understanding Cancer*. New York: Franklin Watts, 1993.

Organizatons
Concerned with Cancer

American Cancer Society
1599 Clifton Road, N.E.
Atlanta, GA 30329

Cancer Care
1180 Avenue of the Americas
New York, NY 10036

Candlelighters Childhood Cancer Foundation
7910 Woodmont Avenue, Suite 460
Bethesda, MD 20814-3015

Leukemia Society of America, Inc.
600 Third Avenue
New York, NY 10016

National Children's Cancer Society, Inc.
1015 Locoust
St. Louis, MO 63101

National Coalition for Cancer Survivorship
1010 Wayne Avenue, 5th Floor
Silver Spring, MD 20910

Susan G. Komen Breast Cancer Foundation
5005 LBJ, Suite 370
Dallas, TX 75244

INDEX